Marigold

The Journey Home

Marisa Rosie

With special thanks to:

Heather and David Johnson, my spiritual parents, whose love and belief in me has been a constant encouragement. Their revelation of the Father's love set me on my own journey with Papa.

Heather Johnson for writing the foreword and encouraging the release of my creativity.

The Glasgow Prophetic Centre, whose staff prophesied that "I had a children's book in me." That Holy Spirit inspired word was the spark that birthed Marigold's story.

Alan Gibson whose beautiful illustrations brought Marigold and her friends to life.

Margaret McWhinnie and Peter Haresnape for proof reading and giving me positive feedback in the editing stage.

Frank Kremer for helping with the layout and design to get the book ready to print

Finally and most importantly, thanks to my Heavenly Father whose love continues to transform my life. This book is all about Him, His Son and the Holy Spirit. It is Papa who inspired each chapter and all the glory goes to Him.

Contents

Foreword

It is a delight to write the foreword to this beautiful story. Marigold's Adventures are a joy and will touch your heart. They will open your eyes and reveal to you the truth of the ages. Your spirit will respond with a yea and amen!

This book is for children of all ages – a must for your bookshelf - full of inspiration, leading you to encounter Father, Son and Holy Spirit whilst giving you time to discover your own identity in the reflection of God Himself.

It has been my privilege to watch Marisa being set free as the Holy Spirit has poured the lavish love of Father into her heart. Her soul has blossomed and her life has been transformed as she has come home and rested in her heavenly Poppa's arms.

When identity is secured in God's love we are free to be ourselves.

When God's love is released creativity

is released.

When His love pours into our hearts we live from a place of rest.

Here in Marigold's story, Marisa shares her own adventures in the Father's love. It is a journey that has captured Marisa and she lives to share this truth with all she meets.

This is an easy and a very engaging read, so enjoy and enter into the adventure with Marigold and her friends!

Heather Johnson
Simply His Ministries www.simplyhis.co.uk

Author's Note

Marigold is my rag doll. I have had her since I was a child. Marigold is also an affectionate childhood nickname. So Marigold, The Journey Home, is in part my own story of coming home to my Heavenly Father. Writing Marigold's story has been the fulfilment of a dream, a prophecy and a stepping into my destiny. The revelation of my Father's love has transformed my life as I come to Him as His child and walk in the freedom of sonship.

In writing Marigold, I have been on my own journey of the revelation of the Father's love. As the Father's love has been revealed to me, the eyes of my heart have been opened to discover the width, length, height and depth of Papa's love for me and for you too. As I come home to Him, I can truly be all I am created to be. I am discovering my true value as a child of my Father and can live a life of peace and trust, securely held in His arms of love.

My prayer is that through the story of Marigold and her friends, children and "grown ups" will discover that they are created for love and will come home as children to their Heavenly Papa.

Marisa Rosie
http://marigoldandfriends.blogspot.com
marigoldandfriends@gmail.com
Become a friend of Marigold on Facebook

flow 12.

CHAPTER 1

The Coming Of Starlight

Marigold opened her sleepy eyes and tried
to stretch her long floppy legs. Not easy to
do when you are a rag doll, lying cramped
in an overflowing toy box. She looked up to
the ceiling and tried to adjust her eyes to the
darkness, pushing cars and trains aside, in an
attempt to stand up and climb out of the toy
box. Bernie the Swiss dog growled as she stood
on his nose "Grr, watch out there, Marigold. I
was still asleep, you know."

"Sorry, Bernie, just trying to get out.
You couldn't give me a helping paw there,
could you?"

Bernie nudged his oversized head and gave
Marigold a push upwards. She grabbed hold of
the top of the toy box and pulled herself over
and fell clumsily on to the playroom floor.

Untangling her long legs and arms she sat up,
leaned against the toy box and looked around
in the darkness. It had been a long time since
she had been out of the toy box. It was even
longer since she had been played with by the
children. They were more interested in their

computers and DS or those toys that talked and moved when you put magical, metal things in their backs. Marigold sighed. She couldn't do any of those things, to make her interesting to play with. She had a painted on face and was just made out of the left over bits of material from the sewing box. Her yellow pigtails were from Granny's stock of wool and her dress was rather faded and shabby looking. She did have big blue eyes, but being a rag doll she could only see in black and white, so the world looked rather dull and boring to Marigold.

Marigold looked around her and wondered what to do now she was actually out of the toy box. The playroom seemed so huge and a bit scary in the darkness and for a moment Marigold wished she had stayed within the safety of the toy box. Just as she was thinking how she could get back into the box, a voice spoke out of the darkness, "Hellllllloooooooo"

Marigold jumped, "Who said that?"

"Why, me" the voice said, "I am Starlight. Who are you?"

"Eh, Marigold," Marigold said, still not sure who or where the voice had come from.

"Pleased to meet you," Starlight said. "I am

over here on the bean bag, by the way."

Marigold turned her floppy head and gasped. There on the bean bag was the most beautiful snow-white swan. Her feathers were spread gracefully on the bean bag and she had a look of royalty about her. Marigold stood up and, without thinking, made a clumsy attempt at a curtsey and nearly fell over again in the process. Starlight laughed, "What are you doing, Marigold?"

"Eh, well you look so, so beautiful, you must be very important, so I just thought..."

Starlight interrupted her with a giggle, "Oh no, Marigold, there is no need for that. Now come over here and tell me all about yourself."

Marigold crossed the playroom to the bean bag and sat down beside Starlight. "Well, there is nothing much to say, really. I am just Marigold the rag doll, made from all the scraps of material from the sewing box. Granny made me for her daughter and I used to sit on the bed. Then I was given to the new children but they have never really played with me so I mostly live in the darkness of the toy box. I used to come out in the hope that the children would see me and put me back up on the bed again, but they are not really interested in an old rag doll like me. So, I usually just stay in the toy box with the other toys that have been forgotten. At least we can keep each other company in there."

"Hmmm" Starlight said, thoughtfully "Forgotten toys, eh! Are there many of you in there?"

"Well," Marigold said "there's Bernie the Swiss dog and Mr Jingles the clown, who is made from scraps, like me. Then there is Susie, who is a bear with no legs, Heidi's grandpa, who has lost all his hair and had to have his body patched up quite a bit and there are some other toys too."

"Hmmm," Starlight said again, deep in thought, "maybe we can do something about this. What do you think Marigold? Are you up for some adventure?"

"Adventure?" Marigold said doubtfully, "What kind of adventure?"

"Oh, the best kind, Marigold, to another world where toys are not forgotten and broken toys are mended with love and care."

"Oh, I don't know, does such a place exist? And how would we get there? And I am just a rag doll. Would I really be wanted there? Oh, oh, I don't know." Marigold protested.

"So many questions, Marigold," Starlight chuckled. "We can fly there on my back and as for the other questions you will need to trust me and take a risk. If we are going, then we need to leave soon before the sun is fully up and the human world awakes"

"Well, I don't really want to go back into the toy box, so I suppose I have nothing to lose. Yes. Okay. Let's go." Marigold said rather unconvincingly, wondering what on earth she had got herself into.

Starlight fluffed up her beautiful white feathers and strutted over to the window which she expertly opened with her beak. She had obviously done this before. "Now hop aboard, Marigold, here we go." Clumsily Marigold clambered on to Starlight's back, her cloth hands wrapped tightly round Starlight's neck. "Eww, not so tight there," Starlight choked, "I need to breathe."

"Sorry." Marigold relaxed her grip and tried to stay calm, but her mind was racing with fear, excitement and questions. Where was she going? She had rarely left the safety of the toy box before and never been outside the playroom, except when she used to sit on the children's bed, but that was such a distant memory, it didn't seem real anymore. What lay before her now? Despite all her racing thoughts, Marigold somehow knew that she could trust this beautiful swan she had just met.

Slowly and gracefully, Starlight spread her wings, launched off the window sill, and lifted up into the sky. The first glimpses of the new day were beginning to peek over the horizon and it was quite a sight to see Starlight fly higher and higher with Marigold clinging on to her back. At first Marigold had her eyes tightly shut in fear, but as she felt the softness and the safety of Starlight's wings around her, she began to relax and slowly opened her eyes to look at the sights below. The world was twinkling with the street lights and the first humans were emerging from their houses to set off for work in their cars. Marigold wished, more than ever, that she could see in colour as it was difficult to make out all that was going on in the world below, when everything was black and white. But she was just a rag doll made from scraps, with painted on eyes and a rather shabby face, so seeing in colour just wasn't possible. All of a sudden, Marigold felt overwhelmed and if her eyes could have cried, then tears would have welled up, but that couldn't happen either. Instead, this dull aching pain filled her heart. Oh if only she was a proper toy, made in one of those fancy toy factories she had heard of. Maybe then the children would still love her and she would be sitting on their bed. Marigold sighed. Would it ever change, even in this other world that Starlight talked about?

"Are you all right Marigold?" Starlight asked.

"Ahh, yes, I think so, just thinking and wondering... How do we get to this land, Starlight?"

"Well we fly east until we get to the horizon, where the sun rises, then south until we see a rainbow. Then we have to catch the colours of the rainbow and we will be there before you know it." Starlight explained.

"A rainbow? I have heard of those, but Starlight, I can't see them, the colours I mean. How can I go there if I can't see it?" Marigold started to panic.

"It's okay, Marigold." Starlight reassured her, "I can see it. That's all we will need for now."

The horizon and the rising sun was getting closer and Marigold could feel the warmth of the sun's rays on her face. Somehow that gave her hope that it would be okay and that Starlight would be able to take her to this mysterious land, which as yet had been given no name. The rising sun got nearer and before its brilliance dazzled them, Starlight leaned over and began to fly southwards and soon the faint outline of the rainbow appeared in the distance.

"Okay, we are nearly there now, Marigold. Can you see anything at all?" Starlight asked.

Marigold strained her painted eyes as hard as she could but all she could see was a grey sky, no colours at all. "Nooooo, nothing," she cried. "Oh and I am sure it must be very beautiful."

"It is Marigold, but don't worry. I promise things will be different soon for you." Starlight said tenderly.

The rainbow got brighter and brighter, its colours radiating warmth and hope as Starlight approached. Red, orange, yellow, green, blue, purple, the colours grew stronger and stronger and then, taking a deep breath Starlight dived into their depths. The colours swirled around Starlight and Marigold and although she couldn't see the colours, Marigold could feel their power pulling them into a strange new land.

CHAPTER 2

Looking For clues

Back in the toy box, Bernie the Swiss dog was
stirring. He was feeling decidedly grumpy
after being rudely awakened by Marigold in
the middle of the night. He rubbed his head
with his paw and was sure there was a rag doll
shaped impression on his forehead from where
Marigold had trod on him. None of the other
toys were awake yet but Bernie could see that
Marigold had not come back into the toy box
yet. He rubbed his eyes and looked around,
then carefully climbed over a pile of cars so he
could look over the top to see what Marigold
was doing in the playroom.

"Marigold, Marigold, where are you? What
are you doing out there?" Bernie said in a half
whisper, so he didn't wake the other toys.
There was no answer. Bernie looked around
the playroom but Marigold was nowhere to be
seen. "Marigold, stop hiding! Where are you?"
Bernie tried again "Okay Marigold, very funny,
you win hide and seek, now come... Oh! Oh!"
Bernie stopped in his tracks as he noticed the
open window. "Oh no, Marigold, what have you

done?" Bernie sighed and jumped out of the toy box to take a closer look. Up at the window he sniffed all around and peered out in to the distance, trying to work out what had gone on in the hours before. Bernie was an expert in these matters. Being a Swiss dog, he was made especially to find people who were missing, although usually they were lost under a pile of snow. He carefully sniffed at the window sill and could definitely pick up Marigold's scent there. But wait. There was something else there too! What was it? Bernie scratched his head. That was most unusual. He could detect a second scent, but not one he recognised at all. This was going to require help, Bernie thought, and turned back towards the toy box.

"Wake up, wake up everyone. We have an emergency here," Bernie barked into the toy box.

"Eh, what time is it?" said Susie. "What's happening?" asked Grandpa. "I was having a lovely dream," mumbled Mr Jingles.

"Marigold is missing and it looks like she has been kidnapped," Bernie said gravely. "She climbed out of the toy box at around 5:30 this morning. Standing on my head in the process, I might add. Now she is gone, the window is open and there is an alien scent there too."

"An alien!" squealed Susie, "Oh poor Marigold, taken away in a spaceship!"

"Not that kind of alien," Bernie sighed, "I just mean, I don't recognise it. Now we need a plan to find her and rescue her. So everyone, out of the toy box and let's work out how to go about this."

Mr Jingles and Grandpa climbed out of the toy box and sat on the floor. "Eh, I am going to need some help here," said Susie. "You see, I am a nightie case so I don't have any legs. I need to have a nightie stuffed into my dress so I can walk, or bounce, actually."

"Humph, okay, let me see," said Bernie looking around the playroom. He spied an old towel lying in the corner of the room. "Would a towel do?"

"Yes, that would work too," said Susie.

Bernie got the towel and threw it over the top of the box and after a few minutes Susie emerged with a bounce over the top landing softly on the floor beside the others. The toys gathered together and looked at each other wondering what to do next. Bernie took charge, since he was the one who had discovered Marigold's mysterious disappearance. He did feel a little guilty that he had been so grumpy with Marigold when she stood on his head and a little responsible that he hadn't checked up on what she was doing. She was after all just a rag doll, and not very used to looking after herself and probably would have trusted whoever or whatever had met her in the playroom. Bernie shuddered, trying not to think the worst, but it was a big scary world out there. Not really a place for rag dolls to be alone.

"Clues!" Bernie said decisively, "That's what we need. Clues! Every mystery has clues and we need to find them, to solve this puzzle. Then we should find Marigold." Bernie hoped that sounded more convincing than he felt. "Susie and Grandpa, you search the playroom, Mr Jingles and I will look for clues at the open window.

The four set to work, carefully looking in every corner of the room for any sign that could help them in the search for Marigold. Susie and Grandpa looked under the table and chair, around the toy box, below the rug and in every corner, but there were no clues anywhere.

Bernie and Mr Jingles climbed carefully on to the window ledge to search around the open window. Bernie nudged the window open further to get a proper look and peered down to the ground. And then he saw it! Caught between the branches of the rose bush, a single white swan feather.

"Ah-hah," Bernie exclaimed in triumph, "Got it!"

"Got what?" the others cried in unison.

"The clue! Now give me a hand, Mr Jingles, while I reach down and get it." Mr Jingles grabbed hold of Bernie's back legs and Bernie slowly leant over the window sill towards the feather. This would require some care. If he nudged the branches too much, the feather would fall and be out of his reach and there were the prickly thorns from the rose bush to watch out for as well.

"A little bit further, but slowly," said Bernie. Mr Jingles slowly leant over further until he was nearly off the window sill himself. "That's as far as I can go, Bernie. Try and be quick. I think you have been eating too much Swiss chocolate again." Mr Jingles strained to hold on to Bernie's back legs.

Bernie stretched out as far as he could, nearly there. Just bite the feather with his teeth and, yes, there it is. Holding it firmly, Bernie said, "mm mmmm mm mmmm mm"

"What, Bernie? I didn't quite get that," said Mr Jingles.

"MM MMM MM MMM," Bernie mumbled with more urgency.

"I think he wants you to pull him back in," Susie shouted helpfully from inside.

Mr Jingles pulled Bernie's legs and the two of them tumbled backwards into the playroom, landing in a heap on the floor. They picked themselves up and Bernie held up the single white swan feather with a look of victory on his face. The others looked back at him blankly, wondering what was so special about a bird's feather.

"Well," said Bernie expectantly.

"Well, what?" said Susie, "What is it?

"It appears to be a bird's feather," Mr Jingles offered helpfully, "though I am not sure how that will help us find Marigold."

"Hmm, is it, what I think it is?" Grandpa asked. "I have heard the legends and stories, but never known them to be true. Certainly never come across one before. Surely not. Can it be true?"

"WHAT?" Mr Jingles and Susie yelled, confused and frustrated that they seemed to be missing the point.

"Yes, Grandpa, it is a white swan feather," Bernie whispered quite overcome with emotion. "I too have heard the story and like many have hoped, but have never seen, until now, that it is true. They really do exist."

"Can someone please explain what is so special about a silly feather and what on earth it has to do with Marigold's disappearance." Susie said exasperated.

"Come and sit down and I will explain as much as I know, and Grandpa can fill in what he knows too. We are about to embark on a life changing adventure," Bernie said.

CHAPTER 3

The River Of dreams

Swirling and twirling, deeper and deeper into the rainbow, Starlight and Marigold turned. The colours merged together and soon became a beautiful golden glow that turned into a road that gently set the two adventurers on its path. Gradually the surrounding countryside came into focus, Marigold could see trees and flowers on either side of the Golden Pathway and in the distance could hear water coming from a river. Although she couldn't see the colours surrounding her, Marigold could feel the warmth and peace of the beauty and felt a sense of excitement rise up in her heart, wondering what adventures lay before her.

"Wow, Starlight," Marigold said in wonder, "Where are we?"

"Close to the River of Dreams, which is where we need to head to first. It will take us towards our destination." Starlight said.

"The River of Dreams?" Marigold questioned. "What is that? Where will it take us? What is going to happen?"

"Ah Marigold, so many questions. It will all

become clear when we are there." Starlight reassured. "Come on, let's go."

Marigold and Starlight set off down the Golden Pathway, walking side by side. Marigold wobbled a bit as her legs felt rather numb after the flight on Starlight's back and she was in awe and wonder at her surroundings. Her head was trying to understand all that was happening to her. A rag doll on an adventure. Who could have imagined that? The playroom and the toy box seemed such a distant memory now, although it was only a few hours since she had clambered out of the box. Oh, a thought flickered across Marigold's mind. Bernie and the others would be awake now and know she was gone. What would they be thinking? They must be so worried about her disappearance. Marigold felt a pang of guilt over leaving them so suddenly with no explanation.

"Starlight," Marigold said, "What about the others, the toys in the toy box? I left them so suddenly, they will be so worried about where I have gone. Can we get them a message to let them know that I am okay?

"It is fine, Marigold," Starlight reassured, "You see, this is not just your adventure. Bernie,

Susie, Mr Jingles and Grandpa are very much part of this, if they choose to be. I have left them a sign and if they look, they too can join in the adventure. But we must carry on and let them decide what to do."

The road began to twist round and the sound of the water got ever closer. Soon they could see the glistening river sparkle between the trees and the road sloped down towards the river bank. A little jetty came into view with a boat moored to its side. This was obviously their next mode of transport and would take them down the River of Dreams. Marigold and Starlight walked down to the jetty and Starlight gracefully floated over the edge and landed in the boat. Marigold looked anxiously at the boat bobbing about in the water and tried to work out how best to get herself into it without making a big splash and giving herself an early bath. Carefully she put one leg over the side whilst holding tightly on to the post to which the boat was moored. The boat wobbled and Marigold pulled her leg back hastily and tried with her other leg, going in backwards this time. With one foot safely in the boat, she tentatively got the other one in and somehow managed to sit herself down opposite Starlight.

"All aboard, let's go," said Starlight, leaning over and untying the rope with her beak. The boat gently moved away from the jetty catching the current downstream. The boat didn't have oars, a motor or a sail but it seemed to know the course to take down the river, almost as if it had been waiting for them to arrive.

As the boat bobbed smoothly through the current its rhythmic movement made Marigold feel more relaxed. Soon she felt her eyelids getting heavy and she rested her head against the side of the boat as sleep overtook her. The trees on the bank bowed their branches in the gentle breeze, whispering in tune to the river. Starlight smiled a knowing smile and settled herself down in the boat, feeling a little tired herself after carrying Marigold all this way. Marigold's eyes closed. Soon she was in a deep sleep and began to dream.

Marigold was transported in her dream to a beautiful palace. Inside, the King was in his throne room, looking through his royal records and thinking about how he became King over this huge kingdom. His thoughts were tinged with sadness as he remembered his best friend, who had died, alongside his father, just before he had been crowned. The King remembered his promises to his friend, to always be loyal and true to him and his family. He wondered if any of his friend's family were still alive so he could show love and kindness to them. So the King summoned one of his servants and asked, "Can you find out if there is any of my best friend's family still alive so I can keep my promise of love to him."

The servant rushed off to his friend's dad's house and found one of his servants, and brought him back to the King. The servant came into the throne room and bowed before the King saying, "Your Majesty, I hear you are looking for any relatives of your friend. He has a son who lives in Lo Debar"

"Then bring him here to me immediately," the King ordered.

Marigold stirred slightly in her sleep, wondering what kind of dream this was. The ripples of the water and the trees waving their branches seemed to be whispering the dream into her heart. Her eyes flickered and she was aware of Starlight sitting opposite her. But then she felt the gentle waves drawing her back into the River of Dreams.

Back at the palace the King was in his throne room waiting for the messengers to bring his friend's son to him. He was pleased that he could keep his promise to him and his family. He had loved his friend like a brother and missed him terribly. Soon there was the sound of footsteps coming along the palace's corridor, the big oak doors opened and the servant entered. Behind him was a young man, struggling to keep up as he was only able to walk with the help of two very roughly made crutches. The young man timidly entered the throne room, fearfully wondering what the King of such an important kingdom would want with him. He had vague memories of his father and grandfather. He knew there had been battles and fighting for the throne and that was how his family had died. Was the King afraid that he would try to regain the throne? Had he brought him here to kill him too?

The King rose from his throne and came down towards the young man. "What is your name?" he asked kindly.

"It's M-M-M Mephi, your Majesty," Mephi trembled

"Don't be afraid, Mephi, no harm will come to you. In fact, quite the opposite. Your father, was my best friend and I promised him I would always love him and his family. Now come and sit beside me and tell me your story."

The King and Mephi sat down and Mephi said, "When I was a small child, my father and grandfather died when there was a fierce battle for the Kingdom. My nursemaid was afraid that soldiers would come looking for me and kill me too, so she fled carrying me in her arms. In the panic she fell and I dropped to the ground badly breaking my legs. But because we had to flee and go into hiding, we couldn't get to a doctor and so my legs never properly healed and I can only walk with the aid of crutches. We fled to the town of Lo Debar which is where we have lived ever since, trying to make enough of a living to keep us from starving."

"Hmmm," said the King. "This must not be so. From this day on, all of your land and the land of your father and grandfather will be given back to you. Everything that was yours shall be repaid to you and you will now always belong to my royal household and be a son to me."

Mephi looked in amazement, "But I am

nothing, your Majesty, just a poor boy who can't walk properly. Why would you show such love to me? I don't deserve it."

"Do not say, you are nothing, Mephi," the King answered, "You are a son of my friend and so now you are a son of mine. You shall have everything my sons have and will always eat with us in the palace."

And so it was that Mephi came and lived in the palace as a son of the King of a vast kingdom. He ate the most delicious food at the King's banquet table, walked in the palace gardens and became a true son to the King.

Marigold's eyes flickered open and she yawned and stretched her long cloth arms. Starlight was quietly watching her awaken, with a look of anticipation on her face, as if she knew that Marigold had been dreaming a special dream. Marigold sat up in the boat and looked around her, trying to remember where she was and how she had got there. The dream was still filling her mind and touching her heart, giving her a feeling that she had not felt before. What was that all about?

"I had a really unusual dream, Starlight." Marigold said sleepily. "I don't understand it, I have never had a dream like it before."

"Tell me about it, Marigold, it might help you to understand it. Remember I told you this is the River of Dreams and the dreams you have here are always especially for you and have a message that is just for you."

"Hmmm," said Marigold scratching her head thoughtfully.

After thinking about the dream for a few moments, Marigold told Starlight all about the King in his palace and how he searched for a relative of his best friend to show love and kindness to. She recalled how Mephi had been found, that he had been injured and had lived a life in hiding, fearful and poor. But, then the King made him like his own son, giving him all the luxuries and safety of the palace. So Mephi became a true member of the royal family. Marigold sighed, "I can see I am a bit like Mephi because there is nothing special about me and I have been hiding in the toy box with no-one to love me. I suppose, also, just as he can't walk properly, I can't see properly, because I am just a rag doll. But, I don't know of any King who would look for me and make me part of his family, so I suppose it was just a dream."

Starlight smiled and said "And what about me, Marigold? Didn't I come and find you and bring you on this adventure? We are not at the end yet."

Before Marigold had a chance to respond the boat had reached the river bank and had pulled up alongside another jetty. Starlight threw the rope over the post and hopped out of the boat. "Come along, Marigold, there is much more ahead."

CHAPTER 4

Swan Feathers

Back in the playroom the toys settled themselves down, all eyes on Bernie, waiting for an explanation for the mysterious, white swan feather. Bernie laid the feather on the floor in the middle of them. Clearing his throat in a self important way, Bernie began regally, "Swan feathers are very rare, so rare that I have never actually seen one before, but I have heard enough stories to recognise one. So I have no doubt that this is a real swan feather. The story goes that this swan is not just any old swan but is a special creature, sent as a messenger. They come looking for a specific person, someone who has been specially chosen and once they have delivered their message they take that person off to a new land. They always leave behind a single white swan feather to be found by the person's friends. It is said that those who find the feather are also chosen and can join the adventure, if they choose to do so."

"Wow," the others said in unison. "But where is his land and what is it like?" asked Susie, curiously.

"Well," Bernie continued, "Of that I am not exactly sure, never having been there myself. But I have heard that it is a place of discovery, with a beautiful river and magnificent trees and that in the middle of the land there is a grand palace where the most powerful King lives. It is said that he is the maker of all things and that he loves like no other. Many people have heard of this King but not many people really know him. He has many people who serve him and work in his kingdom but this King really wants people to be part of his family and live with him in the palace. It is said that anyone can come into his palace and be part of his family but not many choose to do so."

"And this is where Marigold has gone, is it? So is she going to live in the palace? What about us? Can we go there too?" The others fired questions at Bernie.

"It certainly looks like the swan has come and invited Marigold to come with her. And obviously Marigold has gone, but as for the rest that will depend on Marigold and what choices she makes along the journey. According to the stories, living in the palace is an invitation that needs to be received and accepted. The

King will never make anyone come and live there with him. Each person needs to discover his love for themselves and then decide if they want to receive it and become part of his family."

"Surely everyone would want to go and live in a palace! Why would anyone not want to go? And you suddenly seem to know a lot about this, Bernie. How is that?" Susie asked, amazed that anyone would turn down such an incredible invitation.

Bernie looked a bit sheepish and went very quiet for a moment. Eventually he took a deep breath and said, "Well... um... I... you see... a long time ago now I received one of these invitations from a swan. It came to visit me when I worked in the mountains rescuing people who were lost in the snow. And well, I am ashamed to say it now, I thought I was far too important in my job and since that was all I had really, I didn't want to give that up. You see when I rescued people and they owed their life to me, it made me feel good, like I was someone special and I didn't want to lose that. I guess I was scared, so I told the swan I didn't want to meet this King. I was a bit scared as well, wondering what the King was really like. Was he really so full of love as I had heard? I didn't want to take a risk back then."

The rest of the toys weren't sure what to say at this news. They had all known Bernie a long time but none of them had ever heard Bernie mention anything about him having had a visit from a swan. Neither had he ever told stories of the mysterious land and its King before. All of them had heard plenty of stories from Bernie about his mountain adventures. They had all heard how he had single handedly stopped avalanches and dug people out from under tonnes of snow. Bernie had told them all about the medals he had received for bravery and the many times he had found people lost in blizzards, when everyone else had given up. To be truthful, the toys weren't sure how many of Bernie's adventures had actually happened and how many were just made up to make him seem more important than he really was. Susie and Mr Jingles were not really sure if they should now believe Bernie and his tale of this amazing King and his palace. It all seemed to be a little too good to be true.

Bernie eyed them cautiously, wondering

what they were all thinking. He was feeling a bit scared now he had told them so much about his past experience with the swan. He had never mentioned the visit to anyone before and had tried not to think about it. However, there was always a part of him that had regretted not going with the swan and wondered what might have been. That was especially the case in recent times, now that he was no longer a mountain rescue dog and had found himself thrown into the toy box to be forgotten like the rest of the toys. His work in the mountains no longer seemed so grand and important as it once had.

After what seemed like an age of silence, Grandpa finally piped up, "Well, Bernie, who would have thought it. So you have seen swan feathers before."

"Yes," Bernie admitted, "Sorry about that, I just, well, it took me by surprise to discover it. I never thought I would see another, you know, get a second chance, maybe."

"Is he telling the truth, then?" Mr Jingles asked, "I mean about the King and the palace and that he is looking for a family? Is that all true?"

"I certainly hope so," said Grandpa, "I have heard the stories too but never had any experience myself so I can't say for sure. But I suppose there is only one way to find out and that is to take a risk. That is if Bernie wants to and you too, Susie and Mr Jingles."

"Well, I am overwhelmed that I might have a second chance to find the King and I don't want to miss it again," said Bernie decidedly. "I'm in" said Grandpa. "Me too," Mr Jingles said. "Me three!" Susie squealed.

"So what now? How do we find the King and Marigold for that matter?" Grandpa asked.

"Well, Marigold flew away with the swan, but we can't do that because we only have one feather. But the feather was left for us to find so there must be another way for us to follow them," Bernie said, thinking out loud. "Oh, I wonder," Bernie suddenly jumped up. "When the swan visited me before and I decided not to go with her, she left me something, in case I ever changed my mind."

"What was it?" asked Susie.

"A parchment, all rolled up and tied with a bow. I kept it but have never opened it," Bernie said excitedly, "Now where is it?"

Before the others could say anything, Bernie had leapt off the floor and was back in the toy box digging like he was back in the mountains, trying to find people lost in an avalanche. Soon trains and cars came flying out of the box and the others had to dive for cover so as not to be hit by the flying missiles. Bernie was making comments like "in here somewhere," and "ow, that hurt" and then finally "ah-hah, got it!" Bernie emerged with the roll of parchment between his teeth and rejoined the others back on the playroom floor. He put the parchment on the floor and rolled it out so they could read what it said. The parchment had some very fancy writing on it and at the bottom was a map. It read:

Into whose hands this parchment falls,
To them a great adventure calls.
To find a place where you belong,
Where you can sing your true heart song.
Where love is pure and love is kind,
A loving family there you will find.
So take this map to come find me,
And a whole new life you soon will see.
signed with love from Papa

Into whose hands this parchment falls,
To them a great adventure calls.
To find a place where you belong,
        Where you can sing your true heart song.
Where love is pure and love is kind.
A loving family there you will find.
So take this map to come find me.
And a whole new life you'll soon see   Signed with love from
                                            Papa.

N

Rainbow

River of Life

Waterfall

flow12

The map underneath showed the rainbow that Marigold had flown through. From there was a road leading to the River of Dreams and some very big unusual looking trees. It all led to a palace surrounded by gardens filled with flowers, trees, the river and waterfalls. It looked beautiful even just on the map, so what would it be like in real life?

"But how do we get there?" said Susie thinking that she would get very tired if she had to bounce all the way there.

"Maybe we just start walking and the map might show us as we go," suggested Bernie.

"I guess so," said Mr Jingles, "I can't think of a better idea."

So Bernie, Susie, Mr Jingles and Grandpa hopped up on to the window ledge. Bernie went first and jumped down on to the ground so he could help the others down. Once they were all safely in the garden, they started to walk towards the gate. Sitting in the path was a little red car, the one the children had played in when they were little and had sped up and down the hallway, pretending to be racing drivers.

What is that doing there?" asked Grandpa, "I

thought that had been given away a long time ago, once the children had grown too big to sit in it."

"Maybe it is back for us to use," Bernie said. "Let's get in and see what happens"

The four of them piled into the little red car, Bernie in the driver's seat, with Grandpa next to him and Mr Jingles and Susie in the back. Bernie gave the swan feather and the map to Grandpa to hold and began to pedal the car. As he did so, the strangest thing happened. The car seemed to come alive and suddenly took off down the path. When it had enough speed, it launched into the air like an aeroplane and flew off in the direction of the rainbow. Up and up they went, higher and higher, off in the same way that Marigold had gone earlier on Starlight's back. Soon the rainbow came into view and the four new adventurers swirled into its colours.

CHAPTER 5

The Everlasting Tree

Marigold and Starlight headed down the Golden Pathway that ran alongside the River of Dreams. The Golden Pathway was lined on both sides with the most beautiful trees, which were all laden with the most amazing fruit she had ever seen. The tree's branches reached over the Golden Pathway like a canopy. Marigold looked around in wonder at the beauty surrounding her, her mind still full of the dream she had had whilst on the river. Her heart was stirring and bubbling with a strange excitement, mixed with some fear of what lay ahead. Above them, birds were singing a beautiful melody and their song seemed to call them down the Golden Pathway towards their destination.

The Golden Pathway twisted and turned and as they walked, Marigold's thoughts began to race. Why was she here? What was she thinking about, leaving the safety of the playroom? How stupid to think that she could have a new life! Maybe she should say to Starlight that she wanted to go back to the playroom. This was all too scary, too new. It would be better to go back and hide in the darkness of the toy box, than to be here not knowing what was going to happen.

Marigold began walking more slowly as fear gripped her heart. Suddenly the beauty around her seemed to fade and the forest which at first had been so beautiful seemed to close in around her. Marigold sank more deeply into her own thoughts and she remembered how she had hoped before for a different life, only to be disappointed. When Granny had made her and given her to her daughter, at first it had been wonderful as the little girl had loved and hugged Marigold, taking her everywhere with her. But then the little girl grew bigger and began to lose interest in her, leaving Marigold alone on the bed all day. She would still come back at night and hug her but before long, even that stopped and Marigold often found herself thrown out of the bed and left lying on the floor.

The little girl seemed to forget all about Marigold and soon Granny put her away in a box in the attic where she had stayed in total darkness for many years. But then, one day, the box was opened and the little girl, who was now a grown up and a mum herself was there looking at Marigold. She had picked her up with a shout of "Oh Marigold, so lovely to see you," and had taken her downstairs and given Marigold to her own daughter. Marigold's heart was filled with hope that she would be loved again. Unfortunately, things didn't turn out that way as this little girl had loads of fancy toys and soon lost interest in an old rag doll. After all, Marigold didn't do anything fancy or clever. The little girl was sometimes mean to Marigold, saying she was a stupid, boring doll and trod on her when she was lying on the bedroom floor. Eventually, Marigold found herself in the darkness of the toy box, which is where she had been until Starlight arrived.

All of this was whirring around Marigold's mind as they walked along the Golden Pathway. Marigold felt very afraid that this would happen again. She felt sure that when they got to their destination, no-one would want her and she would be left all alone again.

Just then they came to a clearing in the forest and the Golden Pathway opened up to reveal the largest and most beautiful tree Marigold had ever seen. The tree had fruits of every kind possible hanging off its strong branches and was covered in deep green leaves. Marigold stopped in front of the tree and asked, "What is this tree, Starlight? It is so beautiful, I have never seen anything like it before."

"This is the Everlasting Tree and it is the next stop on your journey. Here you must decide if you want to go on further or if you want to go back to the toy box."

Marigold gasped and looked at Starlight, wondering if she had known what Marigold had been thinking. Starlight said nothing more and instead went and sat down at the side of the clearing, leaving Marigold standing before the tree, wondering what to do next. Something in Marigold's heart felt like running away and she turned to look at Starlight, but she had her eyes closed, already asleep. Maybe she could sneak away back into the forest to hide. A deep sadness was filling her heart and Marigold felt so alone.

Suddenly Marigold heard a noise. Footsteps were coming down the Golden Pathway. Marigold panicked and looked around her, on the other side of the clearing was a big bush that would be a perfect hiding place. Without thinking any more she ran over to the bush and crawled under its branches pulling its leaves around her so she was completely hidden from sight. Marigold wasn't sure what to do next, but thought she needed to wait there until whoever was coming had passed by. The footsteps got closer and Marigold pulled herself back, further into the bush so she was completely hidden from sight. A man approached and he looked around as if he was expecting to meet someone. He noticed Starlight sleeping still, so he looked around again, waiting. After a few moments he said, "Marigold, why are you hiding?"

Marigold jumped in fright, not sure what to do. How did he know her name? Had he seen her? Surely not, she was deep in this bush, he couldn't possibly know she was there. Marigold said nothing and lay very still, hoping the man was just guessing that she was hiding and would leave if she stayed where she was.

Again the man said, "Marigold, why are you hiding?" This time he seemed to be looking straight at her. Marigold watched the man closely. There was no anger in his voice, it was gentle and his eyes twinkled with love. Marigold stirred slightly and the leaves on the bush shook, but the man just waited patiently for her to decide if she was coming out or not.

Marigold took a deep breath, slowly emerged from the bush and stood before the man. He smiled tenderly at Marigold and asked her again, "Why were you hiding, Marigold?"

"I ... I was afraid and so I hid," Marigold stuttered. "I didn't know what to do. I thought there was no point going on any further because something bad might happen to me."

"Why did you think that, Marigold?" the man asked kindly.

"Well, bad things always happen, you know. I hope that good things will happen but they never do," Marigold sighed.

The man looked at Marigold and said, "Can I tell you a story, Marigold? It might help you decide if you want to go on further. If, after you hear this story, you still want to go back to the toy box, then that is okay, Starlight will take you back."

Marigold nodded. They both sat down on the grass under the Everlasting Tree. The man began, " A long time ago, at the beginning of time, there was a beautiful garden filled with trees, flowers and every kind of animal. A man and a woman lived in the garden and every day they enjoyed eating the wonderful fruit and walking in the garden. Every day they were visited by Papa, who had made the garden and everything in it, including the man and the woman. Papa loved the man and woman very much and looked forward to spending time with them, talking and walking in the garden. It was a wonderful time. The man and woman were very happy together and loved meeting Papa, laughing and talking and having fun in the garden.

One day the man and woman walked into a part of the garden they had not visited before, where they discovered a different tree that had lovely fruit on it."

"Oh, the Everlasting Tree!" Marigold interrupted.

"No, Marigold, not yet. There is another tree," the man said. "This tree looked so beautiful and the fruit looked really delicious. As they were looking at the tree, a beautiful, shining being appeared and told them how good the fruit was to eat. The beautiful shining being wanted to trick the man and the woman. The woman looked at the fruit and thought how delicious it looked but then she remembered what the man had said. They were not to eat or touch this fruit, because Papa had told him not to. The beautiful being was very sneaky and had been fighting against Papa, so he told her that Papa only did that because he didn't want them to be like him and know everything there was to know. Well, the woman thought it would be good to know everything so she took a piece of fruit from the tree, gave some to the man and they both ate the fruit. After they ate the fruit, a strange thing happened and they suddenly could see the world in a different way. Before, everything had been perfect but now they knew right from wrong. Before, they had been perfectly happy but now they felt afraid and ashamed of what they had done. Before, all they had known was love and peace and safety but now they could see hate and evil and danger in the world and they became sad. Soon after that they heard Papa in the garden, coming to spend time with them, but the man and woman ran and hid because they were afraid of what might happen to them. Papa, came looking for them and said, "Why are you hiding?"

Marigold gasped, and looked at the man wondering what was going to happen next. She realised that she had also been hiding, because she too was afraid, that she knew what was right and wrong and that she felt sad too. She was just like this man and woman! The man paused, looking at Marigold, smiled and asked, "Do you want me to continue, Marigold?"

Marigold couldn't get any words out but managed to nod her head.

The man continued, "After this time, life was never the same. The man and woman now knew all sorts of things about the world that Papa had never wanted them to know and it spoiled their relationship with Papa. They could now tell what was good and what was bad and often chose to do what was bad. It made Papa very sad and it has continued that way all through time. Men and women have run away from Papa and he keeps looking for them because he wants to have that special relationship back."

"How is that possible?" Marigold asked, thinking it was such a sad story.

"Well, there is another tree." the man said.

"The Everlasting Tree," Marigold said, sure that must be the right answer this time.

The man chuckled, "Yes, Marigold, the Everlasting Tree. Papa had to stop the man and woman from eating from this tree so he sent them out of the garden and the Everlasting Tree was hidden away for a very long time.

Then, one day, Papa sent his son to the world to show everyone what Papa was really like. His son was full of love, just like Papa. He taught people that Papa loved them very much and that he wanted them to be part of his family again. Some people believed him and decided to become part of Papa's family but many people were angry that the man said he was Papa's son, so they plotted to put an end to him. Papa's son was put to death and everyone thought that it was all over, but they didn't know the secret of the Everlasting Tree. You see Papa is everlasting and his son is everlasting too. This means that even though he had been killed, he could come back to life again and live forever. Papa's son would then meet people and if they believed that he was Papa's son they could eat the fruit from the Everlasting Tree.

Marigold looked at the man, curiously. "Where can I meet Papa's son?" she asked.

"Ah, at the Everlasting Tree," he replied with a smile and a twinkle in his eyes. "What do you think, Marigold? Would you like to taste some fruit?"

Marigold gasped. Suddenly her eyes could see better. Papa's son had come to meet her at the Everlasting Tree! As they sat under the Everlasting Tree, Marigold was in awe over what she had just realised. This man was Papa's son and he had come looking for her. Marigold still didn't know his name and wasn't really sure who Papa was either, but she knew that she did want to get to know them. There was a sense of safety here with Papa's son that Marigold had never felt before and she felt sure that his Papa would be just like him and Marigold wanted to meet him more than anything she had ever wanted before.

Papa's son seemed to be waiting for Marigold to say something in response to his question. Marigold looked intently at Papa's son and said, "Yes, I would like some of the fruit from the Everlasting Tree." Papa's son smiled and reached up and picked the most beautiful looking piece of fruit from the tree. Before he gave it to Marigold he said, "Marigold, this fruit will change you forever. It means that you are part of our family now and that you will come and live at home with Papa. It means that you believe the story I told you and that you don't want to hide any more. Is that what you want?"

Marigold looked into Papa's son's eyes and knew the answer, "Yes, I want to eat the fruit. I want to belong to your family and live with Papa." Papa's son gave the fruit to Marigold and she took a bite, a burst of flavour exploded in her mouth, sweetness and juice like she had never tasted before. But more than that, as she ate, Marigold realised that she was beginning to see in colour.

CHAPTER 6

Everyone Has A Story

The other four adventurers swirled through the rainbow, the little red car flying through the air with great speed. Soon they had landed on the Golden Pathway next to the jetty where Marigold had been earlier. The car came to a stop and Bernie, Grandpa, Susie and Mr Jingles caught their breath and slowly took in their surroundings. At the jetty there was a boat waiting for them, just as it had for Marigold, so the four of them climbed out of the car and looked at each other and at the boat. Finally Bernie said, "Well, well, that was quite a ride. What now? Is this boat waiting here for us?"

"Why don't we look at the map and see if we can figure out where we are?" Grandpa suggested as he pulled the rolled up scroll from his pocket. He laid the map out on the ground and all four crowded round to see where they were.

"Hmm, well this seems to be the Golden Pathway and this must be the River of Dreams," Bernie said pointing at the river. "I guess we need to go down the river to get to the Golden

Pathway on the other side. That should take us in the right direction towards the palace."

"Oh no, I don't like boats. I get sea sick," Susie moaned, "I still feel queasy after being in the car. And I can't swim. What if I fall in and drown or there might be big fish that will eat me. Oh no, I don't like this," Susie started to cry.

"Well there doesn't seem to be any other way to get across the river. There are no bridges on the map," Grandpa said, rather unkindly. "I think you have to decide, Susie, whether you want to go back or face your fear of the river."

Susie's lip trembled and tears filled her eyes, "I don't want to go back but I don't think I can get in the boat either. I don't know what to do!" she wailed.

"Well, we can't just stay here," Grandpa said, "I am getting in the boat. The rest of you can decide what you want to do yourselves." With that Grandpa strode off to the jetty and jumped into the boat, sitting at the back, arms crossed, with a very grumpy face. Mr Jingles and Bernie looked at each other and then at Grandpa and Susie, not quite sure what to do. Why was Grandpa being so mean to Susie? Bernie nudged Susie gently with his nose. "Come on Susie, it will be okay. I am sure the boat won't sink or anything."

"Oh no, sinking! I didn't think of that! We might all drown!" Susie wailed more loudly than before. "I'm staying here," she said decisively in between wails.

Bernie sighed and looked at Mr Jingles and said, "Well, we can't make her get in the boat. She has to choose. I have to go. I can't miss my second chance." So off Bernie went to join Grandpa in the boat. Mr Jingles looked at Susie and then at the boat, hesitating over what to do. Could he leave Susie here all alone? What would happen to her? She wasn't really able to look after herself. With a sigh he said, "You two go on ahead. I am going to stay here with Susie and we will try and figure out another way to follow you." Grandpa made a "humph" sound, untied the boat from the jetty and he and Bernie gently began to bob downstream, leaving Susie still wailing and Mr Jingles sadly watching them go.

The boat caught the current and soon the two on the bank became specks in the distance. Bernie yawned and tried not to think about what had just happened. He knew from before that everyone has to choose whether to continue on the journey and that Susie and Mr Jingles had to make their own decisions. Sleep began to overtake him, and he yawned again and before his eyes closed, he cast a glance at Grandpa. Grandpa was still feeling grumpy and was fighting the sleep that was trying to take him down the River of Dreams. Grandpa was used to doing things his own way and didn't like it when others got in his way. He had always lived his life according to his own plans, and it had made him a bit hard hearted at times. As a young man his parents had wanted him to work on the farm to keep on the family business, but he had decided to leave home and make his own way in life. He knew it had hurt his parents and he regretted that now, just as he was regretting being so mean to Susie and leaving her on the bank. His heart felt heavy and he stirred restlessly as the River of Dreams drew him into sleep.

Now a curious thing happened, as the River of Dreams took its two sleeping passengers downstream. Bernie and Grandpa began to dream the same dream. But how could that be since the River of Dreams always gives each person their own special dream? Well, although the dream was the same it had a different meaning for each traveller, because everyone has their own story.

In the dream there was a father who had two sons and they lived on a big farm. They had lots of money and the two sons had everything they could have wished for. The father loved them very much and only ever wanted the very best for his sons. But one day the younger son was thinking about the world out beyond the farm. He had heard stories of the big city and how wonderful life was there. He began to feel restless and decided that he would ask his dad for his share of the farm so that, he could go off, explore the big city and have some fun. His dad was very sad at his son's request but, because he was a good father, he knew he had to let his son make his own choices in life. So he gave him his share of the family wealth and the son immediately left on a big adventure.

Grandpa stirred, not really liking the dream he was having and tried to shake himself awake to stop it. He remembered having a similar conversation with his father when he was a young man. He, too, had left home in search of a better life and when he thought about all that had happened to him in the big city, his heart was filled with sadness and regret. Grandpa yawned and moved uncomfortably about in the boat as the River of Dreams drew him back in.

The dream continued with the younger son having a great time in the big city. There were parties and friends and he spent his money having a great time. Life was good. There was no-one to tell him what to do. He could do what he wanted, when he wanted. Soon, though, the dream changed. The younger son had no money left and his friends didn't seem interested in him now he couldn't buy them lots of drinks and take them out to fancy restaurants. Hard times came and the younger son was soon living on the streets, looking for a job. The only one he could find was on a farm, feeding pigs, which was a decidedly smelly job. Soon he was wishing he was back on his father's farm. As things got worse and he became hungrier and smellier, he finally decided to go home and tell his father how sorry he was and ask if he could work for him on the farm. After all his father was always kind and generous, even to the servants.

Then the dream changed back to the farm where every day the father would walk down to the edge of his property and look into the distance, always hoping that he would see his younger son on the road, coming home to him. Day after day, month after month he waited but he never lost hope that eventually his boy would come home. Then one day, far in the distance, a lone figure appeared, walking slowly towards the farm. The father strained his eyes to see. Could it be him? It was hard to tell, as this figure looked so ragged and so much thinner than his son had been.

As the figure came nearer, the father knew without any doubt that it was his long lost son and without further ado he ran and ran as fast as he could towards his boy. When he got to him, he flung his arms around him and showered him with hugs and kisses not even noticing the piggy smell that came from his son. He didn't hear any of his son's prepared speech. Instead he got some fine, new robes for him to wear and new shoes for his feet. Then the father invited all the family and neighbours and threw the biggest party ever, to welcome his son home.

Grandpa woke with tears streaming down his face. The dream was like his life story except he had never gone back home to his parent's farm. He had been too proud and had spent his life struggling to survive on his own. His own parents had died a long time ago and Grandpa wondered who the father in the dream was. Could this be Papa, the one who had signed Bernie's parchment and could he be waiting for Grandpa to come home?

Meanwhile Bernie had been having the same dream but his dreaming had taken a different turn. Bernie's dream stayed on the farm with the older son who had watched his younger brother disappear with the family fortune. The older son had felt very angry at the way his brother had treated their father, so he decided that he would stay on the farm and work very hard for him. Day after day, month after month and year after year the older son worked every day for his father. The older son didn't know how to have fun and he thought that his work was the most important thing. He believed that the harder he worked the more his father would love and accept him. Every day the older son saw his father looking for his younger son.

The older son grew angrier and angrier and worked harder and harder. When the younger son eventually came back and the father threw the biggest party ever, the older son stomped his feet and refused to join in the celebrations. When his father came out to ask what was wrong, the older son complained about all the hard work he had done without any thanks or parties and said how unfair it was for his father to throw a party for his good-for-nothing son. The father looked sadly at his older son and said, "Didn't you realise that everything I have belongs to you and you didn't have to work so hard for me. I love you because you are my son. You could have had a party any time you wanted."

Bernie started to wake up and memories of how hard he had worked as a rescue dog came flooding back into his mind. He recalled his endless work and his anger when people didn't even thank him when he saved their lives. He had thought that working and serving was so important, in fact the only important thing, that he hadn't the time to have fun or spend time with his friends and family. If he was honest, he got really angry with those who seemed to enjoy life and get rewards when they had done little or nothing to deserve it. Bernie gasped as he thought about the dream. Maybe he could still join the party.

Grandpa was now looking closely at Bernie but could see he was deep in thought. Eventually he said, "I had this dream, Bernie that seemed to be all about my life."

"Yes," Bernie said thoughtfully, "How strange. So did I." At that the boat reached the jetty and came to a stop. Bernie and Grandpa stepped out of the boat, still wondering what it all meant and what lay ahead.

CHAPTER 7

The Undeserved Gift

Marigold and Papa's son were still sitting under the Everlasting Tree. Marigold was eating fruit and Papa's son was telling her stories about Papa and what he was like. Marigold was desperate to get moving and go and meet him for herself, but his son didn't seem to be in any hurry. Suddenly, in the distance, they could hear voices, slightly raised and animated. Marigold listened. She was sure she recognised those voices. But surely not. How could that be? The voices got closer and closer, until two figures appeared in the distance. It was the unmistakeable shapes of Bernie and Grandpa. Still deep in animated discussion, they didn't seem to have noticed Marigold and Papa's son sitting under the Everlasting Tree or Starlight who was still snoozing at the side of the path.

"It's all your fault. If you hadn't been so grumpy," Bernie was saying. "Well you didn't have to come. You could have stayed with them, you know," Grandpa snapped back. "Oh, so I miss out on coming just because you were being mean," Bernie growled. "You were being just as selfish," Grandpa said. "Humph" Bernie barked. "Humph" Grandpa retorted.

The two were so engrossed in their argument that they still hadn't seen who was watching them, until they were almost in front of the Everlasting Tree. Suddenly, at the same time, they saw Marigold and stopped dead in their tracks, their argument temporarily forgotten. "Marigold" they exclaimed in unison and rushed towards her, picking her up and twirled her round and round. "We have found you. What has happened to you? Tell us all about it. We are so happy you are safe." They fired endless questions at her, not giving her any time to answer and seemingly still not really noticing Papa's son, who was standing by watching the reunion. After the questions, squeals and hugs had subsided, Marigold said, "I do have so much to tell you but the most important thing is that I have met Papa's son and he is going to take me to meet Papa." Bernie and Grandpa looked over, finally acknowledging that Marigold had company.

Papa's son smiled and said, "Welcome Bernie and Grandpa, it is great that you have come. I have been waiting for you. But tell me where are the others? Didn't they come with you?" Bernie and Grandpa went very quiet and shuffled about rather uncomfortably. Finally Grandpa piped up, and, looking a bit red in the face, said, "It was all my fault. Susie was scared of the boat and didn't want to get in. I wasn't very nice to her, so I left her on the riverbank." Bernie said, "I was as much to blame. I didn't try to help her and could only think of myself and getting what I wanted so I left Mr Jingles there with her to try and help her. I am very sorry." "Yes, I am sorry too," Grandpa replied.

Papa's son stepped forward and took Bernie and Grandpa by the hand and said, "Don't worry! We can sort this out. Now come and sit with Marigold under the Everlasting Tree. Papa's son led the three of them under the tree's branches and sat them down on the ground. Then he went over to Starlight and gently nudged her awake and filled her in on the recent events. Starlight nodded and fluffing up her feathers soared up into the air and flew off in the direction of the River of Dreams. Papa's son went and joined the others, and sitting down beside them, began to talk with Marigold, Bernie and Grandpa as they shared their experiences so far.

Meanwhile back on the river bank, Susie was wailing. She had been wailing for a long time and seemed quite unable to get herself out of her distress. Mr Jingles was pacing up and down, one minute feeling quite overwhelmed at Susie's distress and then fuming at the others for abandoning them on the river bank. He stomped up and down. How dare they leave them there, excluding them from the adventure like that! What was he supposed to do? How selfish! How mean! Poor Susie! Poor Mr Jingles! Left behind, abandoned, rejected, excluded, it just wasn't fair! Up and down he paced, with every wail from Susie increasing his stomping and fuming temper.

"Oh Susie," Mr Jingles finally said, "We really have to do something. We can't stay here on the riverbank forever. Do try to stop crying."

Susie looked up at Mr Jingles, her eyes looking very red and puffy, and through sobs she asked, "What are we to do? Where do we go from here? I am so sorry Mr Jingles for causing all this bother."

"It's okay, Susie. We will work something out. Maybe we should get back in the little

red car and see if it can take us on further."
Mr Jingles suggested.

"Oh, I suppose so" Susie said uncertainly.

Mr Jingles came and took Susie by the hand
and helped her into the car, Susie still sniffing
and trying to swallow back the tears. The two
of them sat in the car, with Mr Jingles in the
driver's seat. He put his foot on the peddle and
the car slowly moved forward down the Golden
Pathway. Unsure as to whether they were going
in the right direction, but not wanting to add
to Susie's distress, Mr Jingles whistled a happy
tune as they drove along the road.

The Golden Pathway followed the River of
Dreams downstream for a couple of miles and
then it began to wind round to the left away
from the river and into more open countryside.
Mr Jingles worried that this was going to
take them further away from the direction
that Bernie and Grandpa had gone, but as
there was no other road to follow, Mr Jingles
kept peddling. Continuing down the Golden
Pathway, Mr Jingles suddenly became aware
of music playing in the distance, and then the
sound of voices and laughter. As they got closer
they could see something in the distance, that

looked like a carnival or circus. There were big tents, and what looked like fairground rides with squeals of happy people coming from them. Mr Jingles gasped, a sudden pang of pain touching his heart. It was a long time since he had been a clown in the circus but the memories were as clear as if it had been yesterday.

"Look Susie, a fairground, I wonder if we can find someone to help us here and point us in the right direction. At least we can stop off and have a bit of fun," Mr Jingles encouraged. Susie looked up and a faint smile came over her face. "Yes, that would be nice," she sniffed. The car drove around the corner and the entrance to the fairground came into view. Mr Jingles peddled hard and the little red car picked up speed, driving into the fairground. They parked the car at the side and Susie and Mr Jingles hopped out of the car, taking in their surroundings. The fairground was full of people enjoying themselves on the multitude of rides, and trying to win prizes by knocking coconuts from their stands. All kinds of performers were entertaining the crowds with amazing feats of juggling and acrobatics and the smell of hot dogs and candy floss filled the air.

The two friends walked around, laughing at all the sights before them, forgetting for the moment that they were lost and were trying to finds the others. Ahead of them was a stage where a crowd was gathering, ready to watch a play that was about to begin. Mr Jingles and Susie went over, curious to see what was happening and, finding seats, settled down to watch the performance.

The curtain opened and a King came on to the stage accompanied by his servants. The King didn't look very happy and he said to his servants, "I can see from my accounts that one of my servants owes me a large sum of money. He has never repaid it. Go and fetch him and bring him to me so I can get my money back." The servants ran off the stage, quickly returning, dragging another servant in front of the King.

"Give me back the money you owe me." the King ordered.

The servant said, "I cannot pay back such a huge sum, your Majesty."

The King then ordered that the servant, his

wife and children and all his belongings be sold to pay back the debt. The servant fell to his knees and begged the King to have mercy on him and give him more time to pay back all he owed. The King thought about this and considered how much the man owed. He felt sorry for his servant so said, "Very well, I will forgive you for the debt you owe me, and let you go free." The servant jumped up with joy and ran off, very happy that he had been forgiven.

Mr Jingles watched the play and his thoughts went back to when he had run away to join the circus. He had stolen money and his dad's car and left without a word. It had hurt his parents very much as they had wanted him to live close to them and work in the family business. His parents had really needed his help but Mr Jingles could only think of himself and what he had wanted at that time. He had such fun being a clown in the circus that he hadn't considered how his parents had felt. His parents though, were good parents and after some time they came to the circus to see Mr Jingles perform and gave him the biggest hug, forgiving him for running away and joining the circus. Mr Jingles knew what it meant to be forgiven for a big debt.

The play continued with the forgiven servant dancing across the stage, happy that he was free from his debt. Another man entered the stage and the forgiven man stopped, and his joy turned to anger.

"You there, come here!" he exclaimed, "You owe me money, give it to me now."

"Oh, please, I have no money at all and can't give you anything back." the other man cried, falling to his knees.

"I don't care, I want my money!" the forgiven man demanded and began to choke and shake the man hard. At that moment some other servants entered and saw what was happening and were so shocked that they ran off to tell the King. The King came running and pulled the two men apart and said to the man he had forgiven, "I forgave you for your huge debt, but you can't forgive this man for his small debt to you. So now you are going to go to jail until you can pay back everything you owe." At that, jailers came on and dragged the man off to prison. The play ended, all the characters came on and took their bow and the curtain came down.

Mr Jingles and Susie looked at each other, moved by the message of the play. Mr Jingles heaved a huge sigh and said, "Susie, we need to forgive Bernie and Grandpa for abandoning us on the riverbank."

"Yes" said Susie, "I want to forgive them for leaving us and Grandpa for the way he treated me. I hope we can find them again so we can do that."

"Me too," sighed Mr Jingles. "Well I don't know what to do now. Shall we just keep looking round the fairground, Susie?"

"Yes, I suppose so," Susie replied.

The two of them got up from their seats and turned towards the fairground rides. As they did so, they gasped because, there in front of them was the most beautiful snow white swan. Starlight had found them. How she had known where they were, they did not know, but found them she had. She puffed up her beautiful feathers and said, "So, do you want to come and join the others?"

CHAPTER 8

Love's Long Length

Back at the Everlasting Tree, Marigold, Bernie and Grandpa were sitting listening to Papa's son, drinking in every word as he told them story after story about Papa. They were all itching to go and finally meet Papa for themselves, but knew they were waiting for Starlight's return, who hopefully would have found Susie and Mr Jingles. It seemed like an age since Starlight had gone but Papa's son seemed unaware and unconcerned about the length of time she was taking to return. He was contentedly telling them stories about his Papa. In fact, all he wanted to do right now was talk about how wonderful his Papa was.

Papa's son was telling them how Papa had asked him to come and tell all his children how much he loved them. He said that he was so happy to do that for his Papa because he loved everyone too and wanted all Papa's children to know they were loved. He told them that before he had begun to tell people about Papa's love, Papa had said in a very loud voice "This is my beloved Son. I am really pleased with him."

Papa wanted everyone to know that he loved his son, not for anything he had done, but just because he was his son. Papa's son explained that Marigold, Bernie, Grandpa and all his other children were loved just the same and that they didn't have to do anything to earn love or make him love them more.

Bernie was trying to understand all this and was finding it a bit tricky. Did Papa's son really mean that he hadn't needed to work so hard rescuing people who were trapped under avalanches? Was it true that rescuing people and getting all those awards for bravery hadn't made Papa love him more? The reason Bernie hadn't gone with Starlight in the first place was because he thought he hadn't done enough good to deserve meeting Papa yet. He believed that he needed to stay and work a bit harder and rescue more people. Then maybe one day, sometime in the future, he may feel he had done enough to deserve love. But that day never came! Not until the day that Starlight had come for Marigold and Bernie had gone after her, had he ever considered the possibility of being ready to meet Papa. Papa's son seemed to know what Bernie was thinking and smiling at him said, "Papa saw every rescue you made, Bernie, and every life you saved in the mountains and he is so proud of you. But even if you had never rescued a single soul he still would love you just as much."

As they were talking, suddenly there was a noise from behind the Everlasting Tree. Someone was coming. Everyone turned to look and there in front of them was, none other than Papa! They all knew instantly it was Papa because he was so like his son, and the look of love and joy on Papa's son's face was so clear that Marigold, Bernie and Grandpa were in no doubt that Papa was finally here.

Papa's son said, "Papa!"

"Jesus, my son," Papa exclaimed as they exchanged a huge hug.

"I have come to meet Marigold and to bring her home," Papa explained. "I thought it would be good if you wait here with Bernie and Grandpa until Starlight returns with the others."

"Great," said Papa's son, or Jesus, as they now knew his name to be.

"Are you ready to come home, Marigold?" Papa asked, stretching out his arms towards her.

Without hesitating, Marigold ran towards Papa and he scooped her up in his arms and onto his strong shoulders, and with a smile and wave to the others, Papa and Marigold strode off down the forest track beyond the Everlasting Tree.

"Will we be home soon, Papa?" Marigold asked.

"We are on our way, Marigold, but we still have a bit of a journey to take, first," Papa said tenderly.

As they came around the Everlasting Tree, a little house with an gnarled wooden door came into sight and Papa headed towards it. Marigold was a little confused. This little hut didn't look much like the house she had imagined Papa would live in. Where was the grand palace, with its beautiful garden, that she had been dreaming of on the river? Surely Papa wouldn't live in a broken down wooden house, that was no bigger than a garden shed. Papa and Marigold reached the hut, and Papa turned the rusty handle. The door creaked open and in they stepped.

Marigold gasped, confusion and fear rising in her heart. The inside of the hut looked just like the playroom. There in the corner was the toy box and the bean bag where Starlight had sat was there too. It was just like the playroom. It was the playroom. Marigold rubbed her eyes, and checked again. It was still there! She was back in the playroom. What was happening, had her whole adventure just been a dream? Disappointment began to creep into her heart. It was just like all the other times, when she had hoped for love and a better life and then it all disappeared again. Who was she, a rag doll to think that anything could ever change, that she would ever be loved again? Was Starlight real? Was the flight through the rainbow just her imagination? Was the River of Dreams just a dream? Did meeting Papa's son at the Everlasting Tree really happen?

But wait! Something was different, Marigold realised as she slowly took in her surroundings. Yes, she was back in the playroom, or at least something that looked exactly like the playroom, but this time she wasn't alone. She was still securely held on Papa's shoulders. Marigold pinched herself just to make sure. Yes, Papa was here, holding her.

"Are we really back in the playroom, Papa?

What are we doing here? I thought you were taking me home." Marigold asked, with a quiver in her voice. "This isn't home, this is... this is... where I am alone and afraid. Why did you bring me here?

Papa, gently reached up and lifting Marigold down from his shoulders, he smiled at her and said "Marigold, you are beginning to see that I love you and that I am bringing you home with me. But you need to see that I have always loved you and that I am and always have been with you. I am loving you right now and you can feel that because you can see me with you right now. But what about all those times in your past when you were alone in the toy box, or left lying on the floor? What about the years you spent locked away in a box in the attic, and the times when the children trod on you or were mean to you? I want to show you that I was with you then and was loving you then. That is why we are back here. My love for you is very long. It stretches back to the beginning of time when I dreamt about the day you would be created and it came to be when Granny began making you from the material in her sewing box. Now come with me and I will show you how I have always been with you and have always been loving you."

Papa took Marigold by the hand. They crossed the playroom and opened a door on the other side. As they went through Marigold gasped again, as they were in the hallway of Granny's house now. How did they get there? Papa just smiled and Marigold had a sense that he could walk through time and space like no-one else could and he was letting her do the same so she could see the world in a different way.

Up the stairs they went and into the bedroom where Marigold had first stayed with Granny's daughter. There in the room was a little girl, fast asleep holding tightly on to Marigold! Marigold gave a rather loud gasp and then put her hand over her mouth quickly for fear of waking the little girl.

"It is all right, Marigold, they can't see or hear us. Now look over at the chair in the corner," Papa said.

Marigold squinted her eyes and looked at the armchair in the corner. There was Papa sitting watching them in the room, keeping them safe. Marigold was trying to get her head round how

Papa could be standing beside her and in the armchair at the same time. Before she could ask, Papa said, "I am outside of time. Marigold, you can only be in one place at time. I have always been here even before time began and I can be everywhere, with everyone, all at the same time. I can see the past, the present and the future and am in every part of every day. That is how I can show you that I was with you when you were asleep in bed all those years ago. Now let's go, I want to show you some more."

Marigold and Papa left the bedroom and there before them were the ladders up to the attic. Papa lifted Marigold on to his shoulders and began to climb the ladder. Marigold began to shake with fear as she remembered the dark, musty box she had been shut into for many years. "Oh no, Papa," she cried, "Please don't take me into the attic and the box."

"I am with you, Marigold. Trust me and I will show you that my love takes away fear."

Marigold shut her eyes tightly as Papa climbed the ladder, not convinced that she wanted to go back to the attic. As they poked their heads through the hatch, Marigold could smell the musty dampness of the attic and could already imagine all the cobwebs and spiders that were lurking in dark corners. She opened her eyes slowly and saw the box into which she had been squashed with all the other unwanted toys and tears began to roll down her face. Tears! Wait a moment. Rag dolls can't cry, but her cloth face was definitely wet. Something new was happening to Marigold.

In the attic still, Papa took Marigold over to a little stool and sat down with Marigold on his knees, wrapping his arms tightly round her. As the tears flowed down her face, Papa held her more and more tightly and Marigold felt a warmth beginning to fill her heart. She began to feel safe, the fear in her heart began to leave and an overwhelming sense of being loved and being safe in Papa's arms filled her whole being. As her tears subsided and peace replaced the fear, Marigold opened her eyes and looked around. The attic was still there, it was still dark and musty and she could still remember being shut in the box, but it was different. Now, she didn't feel afraid of being in the attic and the box wasn't a lonely place any more because Marigold knew now that Papa had been with her in the box in the attic and that he had been loving her all the time.

After a while Papa took Marigold back downstairs. They went back to the bedroom where Marigold was now lying on the floor, having been trod on by the little girl. But Papa was there, tenderly picking her up and kissing her softly on the forehead. Then it was back to the playroom, where Marigold was stuck in the toy box, but this time Papa was there right beside her so she was never alone. Bit by bit, Marigold realised that Papa was there all the time. Throughout every part of her life, Papa had been there, loving her. He had always loved her, he was loving her right now and he would always love her.

CHAPTER 9

Mirror Image

After some time just resting in Papa's arms Marigold looked up into his deep, loving eyes. Feeling a new sense of security and safety, Marigold asked, "Where are we going to next, Papa?"

"Well, I think it is time to take you to the palace, Marigold, and to meet up with the others. There is still much more for you to discover."

Papa led Marigold back through the hallway of her old house and back out into the forest. As they walked away from the old shack, Marigold thought of all those dark days of being forgotten and neglected. She realised that where there had been great pain and sadness, now there was a sense of love and warmth and the deep knowledge that even in the musty, spider filled attic, Papa had been there loving her.

Soon, along the Golden Pathway, Marigold could see something in the distance. It looked like a beautiful palace and Marigold wondered if it was the same palace she had seen in her dream.

"Is that where we are going, Papa? I saw a palace in my dream. Is this the same one I saw?"

"That is where we are going Marigold, but it isn't the same palace you saw. This palace is far more beautiful and so much bigger."

Eventually they came round the corner and approached the huge golden gates at the entrance to the palace. As they approached, the gates opened automatically and Papa and Marigold walked through into the garden. The garden was filled with beautiful flowers and bushes and the most amazing smells of roses, honeysuckle, sweet peas and every other beautiful flower you could imagine. There was grass over to the left where rabbits were munching away, having their lunch. Deer stood gracefully by a pool of water and lifted their heads to watch as they walked through the garden. On the right were fields with horses, galloping playfully and jumping over small fences. Everywhere there was the sense of joy, like laughter filling the air and Marigold wondered what kind of place this was. She had never been anywhere that was so... so... so, what was it exactly? She couldn't quite

think what was so different about this place,
but it was certainly a whole other world. Papa
led Marigold under an archway formed by a
beautiful bush, covered in delicate pink flowers,
along a path and up a few steps that led to
the house.

"I want to show you my home, Marigold.
There are some very special rooms here, that
you can visit any time you want".

As Papa took Marigold along the hallway
she gasped in wonder. The walls were full of
photos of children from every country and of all
ages. She looked at the faces of smiling, happy
children covering the walls from the floor to
the ceiling. Then she gasped again. There in the
middle of the wall was her photo and nearby
were photos of Bernie, Grandpa, Mr Jingles and
Susie. Marigold tugged at Papa's hand and said,
"That's me! You have a photo of me on your wall."

"Yes, Marigold, I have photos of all my
children on my walls to show that you are
always in my heart," Papa said tenderly.

Marigold walked hand in hand with Papa,
marvelling at how many children Papa
had. "Are all your children staying here with
you, Papa?"

"No, Marigold," Papa said sadly, "Not all of my children have come home to me yet. I am still waiting and longing for them to come home. But each child is precious to me and my heart aches for every one of them to know the depth of my love for them. Every day I look for each one who will choose to come and make their home with me and be my sons and daughters."

As they talked they turned a corner and at the end of the hallway Marigold could see they were coming to a dead end. There were no doors or anywhere else to go. All that Marigold could see was a full length mirror on the wall at the end of the hallway. As they walked towards it a quizzical look came over Marigold's face. "What is this? Where are we going, Papa?"

"This is the way to mirror image, Marigold. It is time to see who you truly are."

Papa and Marigold stood before the majestic old mirror, made at the beginning of time, when Papa was forming and creating the world for his children to live in.

"Look into the mirror, Marigold, what do you see?"

"I see you, Papa, smiling with love."

"And who else is there?"

"Well, just me, a rag doll made from scraps. My dress looks a bit shabby and my hair is yellow made from left over wool. I don't really like to look at myself in the mirror."

"Look again, Marigold," Papa said tenderly. "Look beyond the image. Look deep into the mirror."

Marigold peered into the mirror trying to see what was there, but all she could see was the poor reflection of a rag doll. She sighed and flopped down on to the floor, her hands over her face.

"It's no good, I can't see anything else there."

Papa bent down and gently lifted Marigold's head, "Look with your heart, not with your eyes. Look beyond what you can see and the eyes of your heart will be opened to see things as they truly are."

Marigold looked again into the mirror, not really knowing how to see with her heart. But as she looked beyond her own reflection, Marigold saw the swirling colours of the rainbow, red, yellow, blue, green, orange, purple, swirling and swirling. Colours, she could see colours! Marigold had begun to see glimpses of colours when she ate the fruit of the

Everlasting Tree, but this was different. These colours were deep and rich and were swirling and dancing inside the mirror.

As she watched, the colours began to take shape until Marigold could see Granny sitting in the playroom with her sewing box. Next to Granny was a bag of assorted material and a collection of balls of wool in a basket on a table. Suddenly, from behind Granny, Papa came into the picture and sat down next to Granny. Granny didn't seem to be aware that he was there but Papa began to carefully select different materials and look at each of the balls of wool. As he touched each thing, Granny then picked up that piece and began to work away with her sewing box.

As the picture moved on, Marigold could see the forming of a doll, her head and body, arms and legs, the pleating of yellow hair and a dress being lovingly sewn together. At each stage Papa was designing and creating this beautiful doll with Granny. Papa's face was animated, full of joy and pleasure as Marigold's creation continued. He carefully held and guided Granny's hand as she painted Marigold's facial features, brilliant blue for her eyes, smiling lips and pink cheeks. Finally when Marigold was formed and made, a beautiful doll, Papa stood back and admired his wonderful handiwork. There was not a single mistake in the creating of Marigold. Papa always created beauty and perfection.

As Marigold watched through the mirror, she saw herself stand up and walk towards the mirror. The image of Granny and her sewing box faded until all Marigold could see was herself in the reflection. Marigold gasped. This time, as she looked, she didn't see a rag doll, faded and shabby. This time she saw a beautiful princess, handmade with love - a unique creation. She realised for the first time that there was no-one else like her in the whole world. She was wonderfully made. Papa had been the one to create her, and he had chosen the colour of her hair and lovingly painted her blue eyes.

Marigold gasped and tears welled up in her brilliant, blue eyes as she realised that she felt different. Something deep in her heart had changed, the eyes of her heart had opened and she could see. It wasn't just that she could now see in colour with her eyes. Her whole heart was filled with colour. She could see herself as she truly was; she could see herself as Papa saw her, her heart was filled with love. Filled with the love that Papa had for her, she could feel her heart welling up until it seemed like it would burst with love and joy. Marigold began to laugh, and she laughed and laughed until she fell over in a heap on the floor. Papa was laughing too, a deep, affectionate laugh that filled the room and filled Marigold's heart even more, so that she laughed even harder.

They were both laughing so hard they didn't hear the footsteps coming along the hallway. Suddenly Jesus appeared followed by Starlight and there with them were Bernie, Grandpa, Mr Jingles and Susie. Finally everyone had come home.

CHAPTER 10

Home At Last

"Welcome home!" Papa exclaimed, seeing
everyone standing in the hallway. Marigold
turned round and squealed with joy as she
saw all her friends standing with Jesus and
Starlight. There were hugs all round, tears and
laughter, with cries of "How did you get here?"
and "Tell me everything!" Eventually after all
the hugging and chatter had stopped, Papa
declared, "This calls for a party!"

"I agree," said Jesus, "with balloons and
streamers."

"And lots of food," said Starlight.

"What are we waiting for? Let's go!" said
Marigold. Everyone laughed.

Papa led the way back along the hallway.
Round a corner, the sound of music and the
aroma of all kinds of food met them. They
followed the sounds and smells towards a large
oak door. As they approached, the door swung
open and they entered a beautifully decorated
room. All kinds of angelic creatures were flying
to and fro carrying delicious smelling trays
of food, laying them on the large table in the

middle of the room. Marigold and the others gasped in amazement at the sight before them. "Is this all for us?" she asked. Papa smiled, and said tenderly, "Yes Marigold, every time a child comes home we throw a huge party. Our home is a place of celebration and joy. We love parties."

Bernie and Grandpa looked at each other sheepishly, remembering their dream. Before they could say anything, Papa continued. "Grandpa, this party is for you too. It is never too late to come home. I have been waiting a long time for you to come home. I have never given up waiting because I love you so much. I have always loved you deeply, even when you were far away from me. Now you are finally home, I am throwing the best party for you."

Grandpa's eyes filled with tears but his heart finally felt at peace to come home at last. Jesus came and gave him a great big hug.

"And Bernie," Papa said turning to him, "yes, of course you can join the party. It is for you too. All that I have is yours and this is your home. You have spent a long time outside, working hard like a servant. I want you to come inside. You don't have to work hard, for me to love and accept you. I have always loved and accepted you just as you are. It is time you learned how to rest and play. Now you are home I want to show you how to just be yourself without performing for approval. But first, you have a party to attend."

Bernie smiled and his whole body seemed to relax, as if a huge weight had been lifted off his shoulders. The responsibility of being a rescue dog, trying to save people, had been hard to bear at times. He had always been so afraid of failure, of not doing enough. It was a great relief to know he didn't have to save anyone again to gain love and approval. Bernie took a deep breath and Starlight unfurled her wings and wrapped them round Bernie's shoulders.

Standing behind the others, Susie and Mr Jingles were watching all this with big eyes, wondering if Papa would say anything to them. "Susie!" Papa said, holding his arms out. "Come and sit with me." Nervously, Susie came to Papa and he swept her up in his arms and sat her on his knee. "You have done so well, Susie. I know how afraid you have been and how hard it was for you to come on this journey. I want you to know how proud I am of you. You are a very beautiful bear and you have a special place in my heart. My love is taking away your fears and you are going to be able to bounce freely now. Papa squeezed Susie tightly and she felt the warmth of his love. As Papa's love filled her heart, she felt safe for the first time in her life. This is where she belonged.

With Susie still sitting on his knee, Papa turned to Mr Jingles. "Mr Jingles, you have learned what it means to be forgiven and how to forgive others. My heart for you is full of love and forgiveness and the past is gone and now you have a new life, at home with me. Sometimes you still blame yourself for your past mistakes and I want you to learn how to forgive yourself and to let go of the past. All I see, when I look at you, is a wonderful patchwork clown who is full of fun and laughter."

Mr Jingles giggled. He thought back to the play that he and Susie had seen. He realised now that Papa was the King who had forgiven him. Now Mr Jingles could be free from the guilt he had always felt for hurting his parents. He was forgiven!

"Now, everyone," Papa said, "come to the

table. It is time to party!" Each of them found a place with their name written in gold. As they sat down, Jesus came and placed party crowns made of gold and sparkling jewels on their heads. As Jesus placed the crowns on their heads, they all felt like royalty. Real princes and princesses! The table was laden with all kinds of wonderful food - some that they recognised and other food that was straight from heaven. It all smelt delicious and tasted even better as everyone tucked in.

Marigold looked in amazement at the scene before her. She still couldn't quite believe that they were all here. All of her friends round Papa's table. Everyone was laughing, eating, drinking and having fun. What a long way they had come since that morning when Marigold had climbed out of the toy box and found Starlight in the playroom. To think that she, a forgotten, rejected rag doll was loved and always had been loved. The thought that Papa had such a special place in his heart for her, that he would come to find her, was amazing to Marigold.

"This is home!" Marigold thought. "This is where all Papa's children belong. Every child has a place in his heart. A place to be safe and free. Home is in Papa's arms, living with him." Papa came and sat beside Marigold and put his arm around her. She leaned against him, hearing his heartbeat. It seemed to be saying "Marigold" in a steady beat of love. Marigold looked up into Papa's deep eyes and asked, "Why do more of your children not want to come home, Papa?"

Papa smiled tenderly and said, "Many of my children don't believe that I exist and try to live their lives on their own. Many think of me as distant and unconcerned about their lives. There are others who see me as an angry Papa who wants to punish them. Some believe that I am their master and they have to serve me to get me to love them. The world has many wrong views of what I am really like. Many children have put up walls to try to stop me getting close. But I love each and every one, Marigold. I am continually calling my children home. I am always finding ways to touch hearts and reveal how much I love them. It is time for the world to see me as I am - Papa, full of love for his children."

Marigold closed her eyes and thought about

all those other children who didn't yet know Papa's love. Papa continued, "Marigold, you have come a long way from the toy box. You are learning how to receive my love. You are discovering that I have always loved you through every part of your life. You know in your heart that I am loving you right now. The love you are discovering for yourself is for others too. As my daughter, you can share my love with others and help to bring them home to me."

Marigold looked quizzically at Papa, but before she could say anything, Papa kissed her forehead. "My love is to flow through you, Marigold. As it touches and heals your heart, you come to know and receive more of my love. Then you can reveal my love to those you meet. It won't be an effort or hard work. When you live close to me, letting me love you, my love will overflow from you to others. Come with me, Marigold I want to show you something."

Papa took Marigold by the hand and led her out of the room, leaving the others still partying. They went up a huge staircase to the top of the palace. At the top was a circular room with a view in every direction. Marigold gasped.

She could see for miles and all in full colour. She could see people and houses, animals and cars, towns and countryside. The whole world going about its business. Some people looked happy, others sad. Most didn't seem to have any point to their lives and were just living to survive each day. All needed to know Papa and how to come home to him.

"There is a whole world out there, Marigold. It is waiting for you to explore. There are many adventures still to come, that we are going to have together. Adventures to take my love to the children out there and to bring them home. What do you say Marigold? Do you want to come on this adventure with me?"

Marigold didn't have to think about her answer, "Yes Papa, I want to be with you. I want to go where you go. I want to know you more and live as your daughter forever."

So Marigold is home at last with Papa. But she knows this is not the end of the story. It is only really the beginning.